EVERGREEN PARK PUBLIC LIBRARY

3 2778 00143 3971

W9-CCE-820

EVERGREEN PARK PUBLIC LIBRARY
9400 S. TROY AVENUE
EVERGREEN PARK, IL 60805

DEMCO

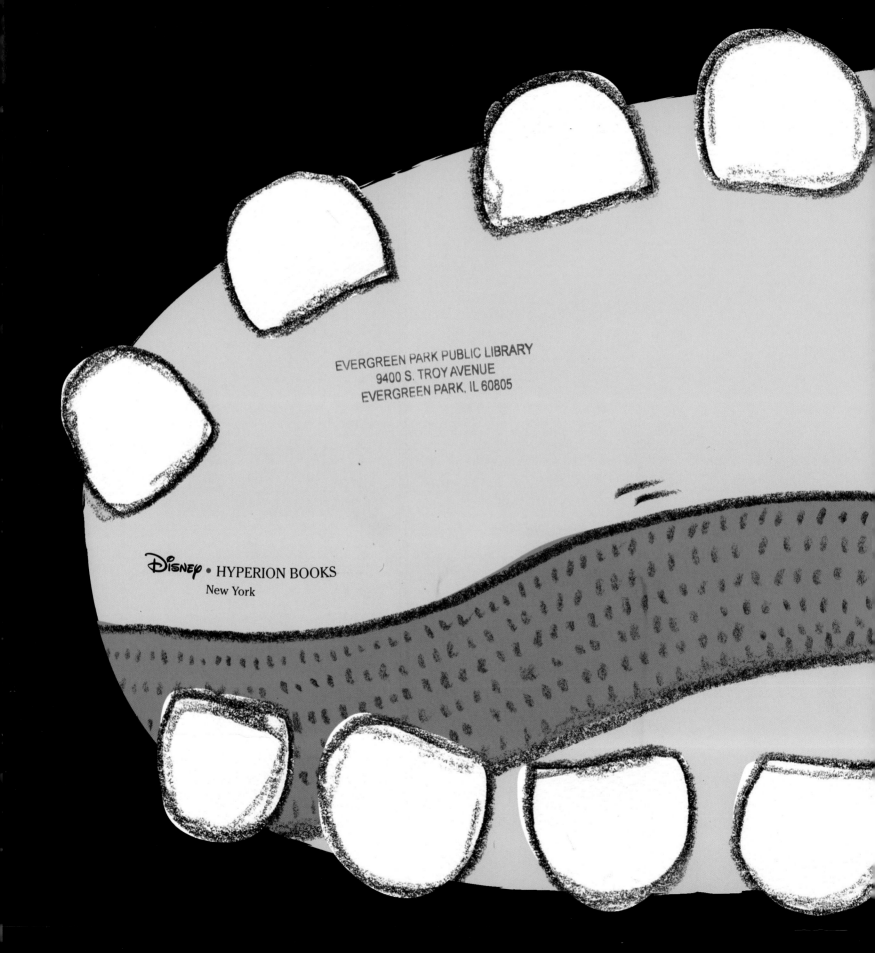

EVERGREEN PARK PUBLIC LIBRARY
9400 S. TROY AVENUE
EVERGREEN PARK, IL 60805

Disney • HYPERION BOOKS
New York

FOOD HATES YOU, TOO
AND OTHER POEMS

ROBERT WEINSTOCK

For Pearl, who I will eat one day

Text and illustrations © 2009 by Robert Weinstock

All rights reserved. Published by Disney • Hyperion Books, an imprint of Disney Book Group.
No part of this book may be reproduced or transmitted in any form or by any means, electronic
or mechanical, including photocopying, recording, or by any information storage and retrieval system,
without written permission from the publisher. For information address
Disney • Hyperion Books, 114 Fifth Avenue, New York, New York 10011-5690.

First Edition

1 3 5 7 9 10 8 6 4 2

This book is set in 14-point Cheltenham.

Printed in China
Reinforced binding

Library of Congress Cataloging-in-Publication Data on file.

ISBN 978-1-4231-1391-1

Visit www.hyperionbooksforchildren.com

CONTENTS

FERRiS-WHEELiNG

Ferris-wheeling is appealing

when your stomach isn't feeling

corndog-whirling, taffy-twirling,

cotton-candy-heaving, hurling,

curling, swirling, kneeling, reeling,

that's when it is most appealing.

Who is up for Ferris-wheeling?

SIDESHOW

I have a hen beyond compare.
See . . . every egg it lays is square.
Not just the shell. Check out the yolk.
All pink-and-purple stripes—no joke.
It tastes like bubble gum, I swear,
And blows square bubbles with blue hair,
With greenish bald spots here and there.
I swear this isn't just hot air.

FOOD HATES YOU, TOO

Nuts!

What kind of name is BRAD??

Zut!

If everyone hates different food,
Then couldn't it be true
That creamed chipped beef dislikes Gertrude,
And liver gags on Lou?

That Brads are loathed by brussels sprouts,
And Genes scare lima beans?
That trail mix tries to flee Girl Scouts,
And tripe can't stand Doreens?

That mayonnaise detests Pierre,
And mustard weeps from Fritz?
That Juan makes sushi gasp for air,
And Atsuko gives tacos fits?

That Trudys gross out rainbow trout,
And Rachels skeeve out schmaltz?
That Tommys make pastramis pout,
And sardines cringe at Walts?

That pickled beets go green from Petes,
And grape leaves blanch at Steves?
That deli meats balk at Brigittes
And Eves give tongue the heaves?

"Big deal," you yawn. "Who gives a prawn
If pitted prunes snub June?
If duck pâté takes flight from Fawn,
And borscht dreads Igor's spoon?"

But what if Jakes gave cakes the quakes?
If Liam made popcorn scream?
If Blakes were feared by chocolate shakes,
And ice cream shunned Hakeem?

If doughnuts hid from Dominic?
If Fern made cookies faint?
If Charles made chewy candy sick,
And Pearl left pudding pained?

If cotton candy, apple pie,
And french fries looked at you
And said, "Gross! Blecchh! Nope, I won't try.
I'll never like it. Ew!"

I'm sure you'd say, "Hey! That's no fair!
Give me a chance! You should
Just try me. Pretty please? I swear!!
With sugar on top . . . ? I'm good!"

ELEANOR ISABEL ABIGAIL RHODA

There once was a tall girl from north South Dakota
Named Eleanor Isabel Abigail Rhoda,
Who only drank orange-grape-strawberry soda.
And nothing else. Never. Not one small iota.

BENJAMIN BENJAMIN DIETZ

Meet Benjamin Benjamin Dietz.

He repeats and repeats what he eats.

He eats sweet-flavored meats,

With his meat-flavored sweets,

And eats beets with his beets with his beets.

TOAST

There was a piece of bread named Ned,

Whose twin bread brother's name was Fred.

They idly lived within a loaf,

Until one day I ate them both.

And now, I'm sad to say, they're dead.

NED
CRUSTY
TO THE
END

FRED
NOBODY
WAS
FRESHER

Crumby
story.

I like
crumbs.

PERNICIOUS

Who cares if a fish is nutritious?
Please tell me if it is delicious!
That fishes eat fishes
Still leaves me suspicious—
What else is there down there, knishes?

Recipe

A pound or two of Arctic char,
Eight dozen medium sardines,
Four tablespoons of caviar,
Six bags of kelp or kelplike greens.

Nine hundred barnacles or clams,
Three thousand tons of humpback whale,
Five million cups of sifted sand,
A pint of shrimp—still with the tail.

Add equal parts of squid and krill,
A pinch of crab, a dash of cod,
A heaping quart of mackerel,
Twelve unminced eel, one unpoached scrod.

Then whisk in zest of coral reef.
Stir in shipwrecks when in season.
The smell is quite beyond belief.
Salt to taste, but within reason.

(Some think this recipe is best,
With hints of sunken treasure chest.)

MOM

I ate your father. Yes, it's true.

That's what we praying mantids do.

His last words to me were "Adieu.

If only I could eat you, too."

INVENTION

Rapunzel and Denzel D. Wenzel
Have invented the strangest utensil,
Which has four tiny tines
That draw parallel lines.
It's a fork! Wait! It's also a pencil!
Eat the smallest of crumbs!
Draw identical plums!
Without thumbs! (This utensil's prehensile.)

CHEESE SONNET

When I was young I smelled like curds and whey,
And lived inside a pail beneath a cow.
Just where I lived before, that's hard to say.
Some say inside a cow. I don't know how

That's true. I'm not a cow. I never was.
But this is not the point. The point's life stinks!
Like feet. Like worse than feet. And that's because
It's me that smells. And no one ever thinks

To ask if all the jokes they tell behind
My back might hurt my feelings. Well, they do.
They might not if I had a thicker rind.
I guess I'm soft—I wish that it weren't true.

But you are hard and mean! So shame on you!
It's totally your fault that I grow blue!

MONDAY

Monday smells like dinner rolls
Or is it buttered toast?
Or maybe oatmeal served in bowls
Smells like a Monday most?

Tuesday feels like lemon peels,
Though sometimes more like limes.
Tuesday also sometimes feels
  Like clementines. Sometimes.

    Wednesday's mostly tuna fish
      In casseroles with peas.
        A gloppy goop all yellowish
          With moldy cheddar cheese.

          Thursday's usually gingerbread
            Or else it's rhubarb pie.
              But could be liverwurst instead
                Of these. Don't ask me why.

Friday is a rack of ribs,

Beef fondue, and sushi boats,

And moo shu pork and plastic bibs

And also root beer floats.

Saturday's like honeydews,

Like cucumbers and kiwis,

Or Southeast Asian rambutans, whose

Juice is sweet like lychees.

Sunday should be filled with jam,

And browned like griddle cakes,

Then sliced like baked Virginia ham,

And rubbed like stomachaches.

21

PUDDING

No more coulding,
Woulding, shoulding.
Make me, mix me,
Fix me pudding!

JAM

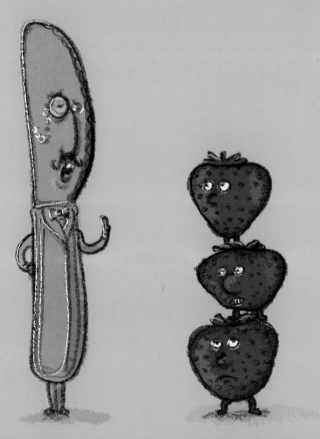

Must I say it twicely?
I've asked you rather nicely.
I need to cram my face with jam,
Don't make me ask you thricely!

DOUGHNUTS

I go nuts for doughnuts,
All tingles from Pringles
And swoony from bacon,
If I'm not mistaken.

FLAVOR OF THE DAY

I'll give you some friendly-advice cream:
Don't order the rat-ripple mice cream.
It sounds good but isn't so nice cream.
Instead try the hair-ball-and-lice cream.

ICE CREAM
PARLOR

NO HISSING OR SCRATCHING

THE BIG SLURP

If I could build a giant straw,
I'd guzzle up the sky,
Plus every star you ever saw.
I would. Just watch me try.

HEAVENLY CONFECTIONS

The moon is not a peppermint.
It isn't made of cheese.
It tastes like dirt and dust and flint—
Like Earth without the trees or seas.

The Sun might taste like lemon drops.
It's just too hot to tell.
It cooks all day. It never stops
To cool enough to taste or smell. Oh well.

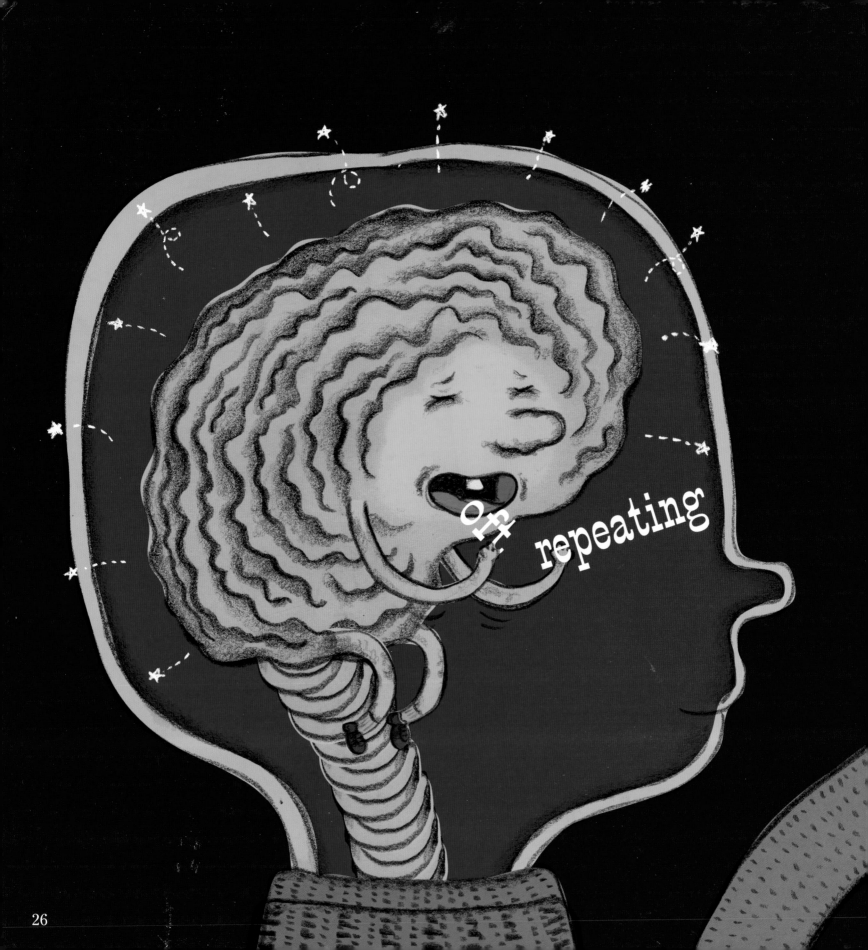